Little Louie
the
Baby Bloomer

BY ROBERT KRAUS

PICTURES BY JOSE ARUEGO & ARIANE DEWEY

SCHOLASTIC INC.

New York Toronto London Auckland Sydney
Mexico City New Delhi Hong Kong

ISBN 0-439-14829-4

Text copyright © 1998 by Robert Kraus.
Illustrations copyright © 1998 by Jose Aruego and Ariane Dewey.
All rights reserved.
Published by Scholastic Inc., 555 Broadway, New York, NY 10012,
by arrangement with HarperCollins Children's Books, a division of HarperCollins Publishers.
SCHOLASTIC and associated logos are trademarks and/or registered
trademarks of Scholastic Inc.

12 11 10 9 8 7 6 5 4 3 2 1   9/9 0 1 2 3 4/0

Printed in the U.S.A.   14

First Scholastic printing, April 1999

Typography by Al Cetta

To Alix and Parker

—R.K.

To Juan

—J.A. and A.D.

Leo's little brother, Louie,
couldn't do anything right.

He couldn't throw a ball.

He couldn't pull a wagon.

He couldn't rattle his rattle.

He was a messy eater.

And he never said a word.

Every day Leo played with his friends.

Every day he tried to play with Little Louie, too.

"What's the matter with Little Louie?" asked Plover.

"Why can't he throw a ball?" asked Elephant.

"Why can't he pull a wagon?" asked Crocodile.

"Why can't he rattle his rattle?" asked Snake.

"And he can't talk, either," said Leo.

Leo was worried.

"Why won't Little Louie play with me?"
he asked.

"Little Louie will play with you in his own
good time," said Leo's father.

"And in his own good way," said Leo's mother.

"He's a late bloomer, just like you."

So Leo stopped trying to play with Little Louie
and decided to teach Louie instead.
Every day he showed him how to throw a ball.

Every night he showed him how to pull a wagon.

He showed Louie how to rattle his rattle,

and he tried to teach him how to say his name.

LE+O=LEO
LEE-OOH
LEO   LEOOO

Leo decided not to teach Little Louie how to eat.

"Are you sure Little Louie is a bloomer?"
Leo asked his parents.

"Patience," said his mother.

"A watched bloomer doesn't bloom,"
said his father.

Then one day Leo got it!

Little Louie had bloomed already.

He could throw.

He could pull.

He could rattle.

He could even eat neatly.

He just did it all in his own good way.

The next time Leo's friends came over, Leo said,

"Little Louie made it!"

"Just like you," said Plover.

"A late bloomer," said Crocodile.

"A baby bloomer," Leo said.

"Except he still doesn't talk."

"Leo!" said Little Louie.